For my children – K.T.

Much love, thanks and kisses to all those who have
supported me throughout Pablo's creation – H.G.

First published in Great Britain in 2009 and in the USA in 2010 by
Frances Lincoln Children's Books, 4 Torriano Mews,
Torriano Avenue, London NW5 2RZ
www.franceslincoln.com

British Library Cataloguing in Publication Data available on request

ISBN 978-1-84507-409-8

Set in StoneSans

Illustrated with watercolour and gouache

Printed in China

1 3 5 7 9 8 6 4 2

Pablo Meets the Neighbours

Hannah Giffard • Keith Tutt

F
FRANCES LINCOLN
CHILDREN'S BOOKS

Pablo, Poppy and Pumpkin were looking out of the den. Pablo could see Finbar the cat sleeping peacefully on the window-sill.

"Why do we live in a tiny hole in the ground, when Finbar lives in a nice big house?" said Pablo, looking out across the garden.

"He must be a friend of the humans," Pumpkin replied.

"Mum and Dad say that foxes can't be friends with humans," said Poppy.

"I'm going to ask that cat what it's like to live with humans!" said Pablo. In a flash he had disappeared through the cat-flap.

"Wait for me, Pablo!" cried Pumpkin, racing after him.

"This is going to end badly. I just know it," said Poppy, following them into the house.

Pablo nudged open a big door with his nose.

"These humans are surprisingly good hunters," he said, looking in the fridge. Pumpkin started chomping on a chicken bone.

"It was very kind of them to leave us all this food," said Pablo.

"Are you sure they left it for us?" said Poppy, looking around nervously.

In the next room, Pablo and Pumpkin discovered a big, bouncy sofa.

"Whoopee!" they cried as they flew through the air. Just then, Pumpkin's tail knocked over a jug of flowers.

"Oops!" said Pumpkin, as the water spilled all over the floor.

"Don't worry, Pumpkin," said Pablo. "Humans LIKE water on their floors."

"How do you know?" asked Pumpkin.

"Oh, I know lots of things about humans," said Pablo.

"Come on, you two – shouldn't we be looking for Finbar?" said Poppy.

"What's behind this door?" Pumpkin wondered.
But when the door opened, a strange beast leapt out.
"HELP, it's attacking me!" Pumpkin cried, as he rolled
around on the carpet, struggling to escape.

"Don't be silly," said Poppy. "It's not even alive."

"It fights well, for something that's not alive!" said Pablo. He helped Pumpkin untangle himself from the scary beast.

"Follow me," said Pablo, climbing the stairs. "It'll never catch us up here."

"Hunting cats is hard work," said Pumpkin, bouncing on the big, soft bed.

"Maybe Finbar's hiding under all this stuff," said Pablo, emptying the washing basket.

"Ssh! I can hear someone," said Poppy.

But Pablo was far too busy to listen.

Downstairs, the family arrived home.

"What a mess! We've been burgled! Call the police!" cried Mum and Dad.

"Maybe it was Finbar," said the little girl.

Soon they were searching everywhere for their naughty black cat.

"Quick! Get out of here!" said Poppy. "Follow me, you two!"

"Good idea," said Pumpkin, yawning.

But Pablo said stubbornly, "I came here to find Finbar. And I'm not going home until I do."

"Then you're even crazier than I thought!" said Poppy, as Pablo disappeared up a ladder.

Up on the roof, Finbar was
sunning himself.

   "What are you doing here?"
he asked Pablo.

   "Looking for you, of course."

   "Well, now you've found me,
you can go straight down again!"

   Just then, Pablo wobbled,
lost his balance and fell down
the chimney-pot.

"Yahooooooo!" cried Pablo, sliding
down the chimney and crashing into
the fireplace.

"Look," said the little girl, as Pablo
tumbled out covered in soot. "It's Finbar!"

"Get that filthy cat out of here!" said
the little girl's mother, waving a broom
at Pablo.

Pablo ran as fast as he could towards the back door.

Poppy and Pumpkin were waiting for Pablo in the garden,
when suddenly something appeared through the cat-flap.

"Have you seen our brother?" Pumpkin asked the sooty
creature. "He's a little red fox, and he was looking for a cat."

"I AM your brother!" said Pablo, sneezing loudly.

"Oh no you're not," said Pumpkin crossly.

Just then, it started to rain.